WASHINGTON, D.C.

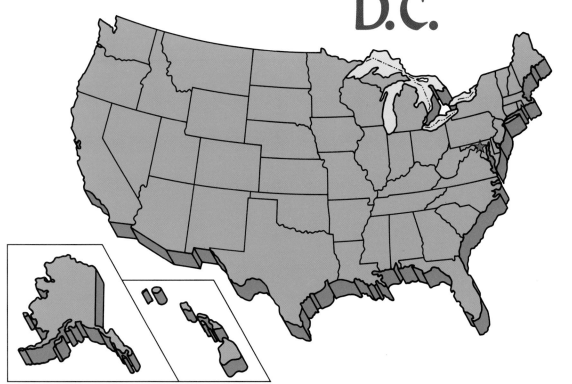

Hello U★S★A★

WASHINGTON, D.C.

Joyce Johnston

★ ★ ★

Lerner Publications Company

LIBRARY OF CONGRESS
CATALOGING-IN-PUBLICATION DATA
Johnston, Joyce.
    Washington, D.C. / Joyce Johnston.
        p.   cm. — (Hello U.S.A.)
    Includes index.
    Summary: Introduces the geography, history, people, employment, interesting sights, and environmental concerns of the nation's capital.
    ISBN 0-8225-2751-0 (lib. bdg.)
    1. Washington (D.C.)—Juvenile literature.
2. Washington (D.C.)—Geography—Juvenile literature. [1. Washington (D.C.)] I. Title.
II. Series.
F194.3.J64   1993
975.3—dc20   92-44848
                                    CIP
                                    AC

Manufactured in the United States of America
1 2 3 4 5 6 – I/JR – 98 97 96 95 94 93

Cover photograph by Mae Scanlan.

The glossary that begins on page 68 gives definitions of words shown in **bold type** in the text.

 This book is printed on acid-free, recyclable paper.

CONTENTS

Did You Know . . . ?

☐ Washington, D.C., is one of the few cities in the world that was planned before it was built.

☐ Rising 555 feet (169 meters) into the air, the Washington Monument is the tallest building in Washington, D.C. When the tower first opened in 1888, the elevator ride to the top was 10 minutes long. Nowadays the ride takes only 70 seconds.

☐ The Library of Congress in Washington, D.C., is one of the world's largest libraries. With more than 80 million items, the library's collection includes books, manuscripts, newspapers, musical scores, maps, microfilm, photos, recordings, and films.

❑ Abraham Lincoln, the 16th president of the United States, was shot at Ford's Theatre in Washington, D.C., on April 14, 1865. Visitors can tour the theater and the house across the street where the president died the following day.

The president of the United States lives in the White House.

❑ During the War of 1812, many of Washington's government buildings—including the president's house—were burned. As part of the repair job, the president's blackened residence was painted white and has been called the White House ever since.

A Trip Around the City

One hundred miles (161 kilometers) up the Potomac River from the Chesapeake Bay lies Washington, D.C., the capital of the United States of America. As the headquarters of the U.S. government, Washington is the city where the U.S. Congress meets, where the president lives and works, and where citizens from around the nation come to express their opinions.

Washington, D.C., is not part of any state. The capital city belongs to a separate district, or section, of the United States. Named after explorer Christopher Columbus, this section is called the District of Columbia (or D.C.). The city of Washington covers all 68 square miles (176 sq km) of the district.

Cherry trees line the edge of the Tidal Basin. This large pool of water lies near the Jefferson Memorial, a monument honoring the third president of the United States.

Members of the U.S. Congress meet in the Capitol building to make laws for the nation.

Washington's neighbor on three sides is the state of Maryland. To the southwest, across the Potomac River, lies Virginia. Washington's metropolitan area, which includes the city and its surrounding suburbs, extends far into Maryland and Virginia. Covering 3,957 square miles (10,249 sq km), the metropolitan area is more than 50 times the size of the city itself.

The city of Washington is divided into four parts—Southeast, Southwest, Northeast, and Northwest. These four sections meet at the U.S. Capitol building, which sits on a hill close to the Potomac River. Known as Capitol Hill, the mound is also the site of the Supreme Court, the Library of Congress, and other important buildings.

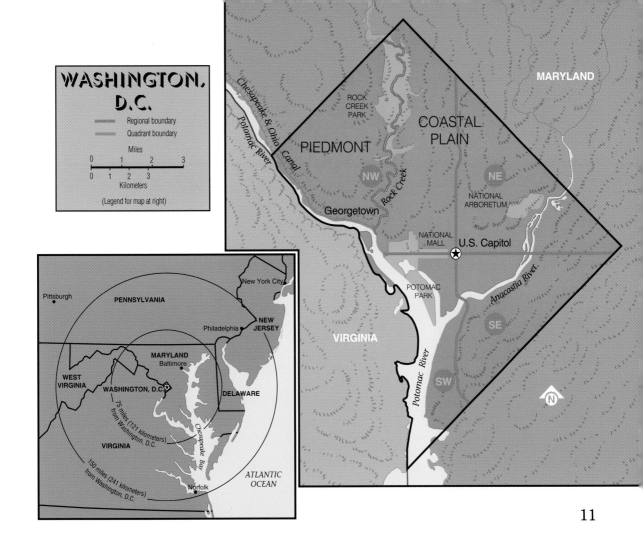

WASHINGTON, D.C.

Regional boundary
Quadrant boundary

Miles
0   1   2   3

Kilometers
0   1   2   3

(Legend for map at right)

MARYLAND

ROCK CREEK PARK

COASTAL PLAIN

PIEDMONT

NW

NE

Rock Creek

NATIONAL ARBORETUM

Chesapeake & Ohio Canal

Potomac River

Georgetown

NATIONAL MALL

U.S. Capitol

Anacostia River

VIRGINIA

POTOMAC PARK

SE

Potomac River

SW

N

Pittsburgh

PENNSYLVANIA

New York City

NEW JERSEY

Philadelphia

MARYLAND
Baltimore

WEST VIRGINIA

WASHINGTON, D.C.

DELAWARE

75 miles (121 kilometers) from Washington, D.C.

Chesapeake Bay

VIRGINIA

150 miles (241 kilometers) from Washington, D.C.

Norfolk

ATLANTIC OCEAN

11

Major Pierre Charles L'Enfant, the man who planned the city of Washington, situated the president's house about 1.5 miles (2.4 km) northwest of the Capitol building. Between the White House and the Capitol is the Federal Triangle, which has more government buildings than any other area in the city.

Parks were an important part of L'Enfant's plan. One park, the National Mall, stretches 2 miles (3 km) from the Capitol building to the Lincoln Memorial. The largest parks in the city include Potomac Park, Rock Creek Park, and Anacostia Park.

Washington's metropolitan area is located on two geographic regions—the Coastal Plain and the Piedmont. Most of the city is built on the low-lying Coastal Plain, which extends east to the Atlantic Ocean.

Parks *(left)* are common in Washington. *The Awakening*, a popular sculpture *(above),* lies in East Potomac Park.

Rock Creek, a small stream that flows through the western part of the city, separates the Coastal Plain from the higher land of the Piedmont. Georgetown and other neighborhoods in the Northwest section of the city lie on the Piedmont. So do Washington's western suburbs.

Waterfalls form on the Potomac River at the point where the high, rocky land of the Piedmont region meets the low, sandy soil of the Coastal Plain.

The rock of the Piedmont is harder than that of the Coastal Plain. Upstream from Georgetown, the Potomac River has been able to carve only a narrow channel through the Piedmont's hard granite rock. Downstream, the river has cut a wide path through the soft earth of the Coastal Plain.

The Potomac River is one of Washington's two major rivers. The other river, the Anacostia, flows south through the eastern half of the city and meets the Potomac at the tip of East Potomac Park.

Washington's climate is mild and moist. About 50 inches (127 centimeters) of **precipitation,** or rain and snow, fall on the city each year. The average temperature in the winter is 37° F (3° C). In the summer, the average temperature is 78° F (26° C). It's not unusual for the temperature to rise above 90° F (32° C) on a July or August afternoon.

With its warm weather, Washington is a good home for many different plants, including the famous cherry trees in Potomac Park. A gift from Japan, the trees produce thousands of delicate pink and white blossoms every April.

Other trees and shrubs from around the world thrive in Washington's National Arboretum, a special park where scientists can study plants. The arboretum is well known for its herb garden, its collection of bonsai (miniature potted trees), and for its flowering azalea shrubs.

Rock Creek Park and Theodore Roosevelt Island are two places in Washington to see wildlife. Gray and red squirrels, cottontail rabbits, woodchucks, muskrats, and chipmunks all live in these natural areas. Visitors might also hear bullfrogs or cricket frogs, or see a salamander slither across a rock.

The bullfrog is the largest frog in the United States. It can grow to be 8 inches (20 centimeters) long.

The colorful blossoms of dogwood trees and azalea shrubs brighten Washington's National Arboretum.

The Story of Washington, D.C.

In 1789, when George Washington became the first president of the United States, the new nation did not yet have a permanent capital city. Several states had offered to donate land for a capital. But Congress, the group of people elected to make laws for the country, could not decide whether the capital should be in a Northern or a Southern state.

A Southern location was finally agreed to one evening in 1790 at Thomas Jefferson's house. Jefferson was from the Southern state of Virginia. His dinner guest, Alexander Hamilton, was from New York, a Northern state. Both Hamilton and Jefferson worked for President Washington.

At dinner, Jefferson promised to persuade congressmen from Virginia to vote in favor of a bill that Hamilton and other Northerners supported. In return, Hamilton promised to urge congressmen from the North to vote to locate the U.S. capital in the South.

In the 1790s, the site of what would become the District of Columbia was mostly farmland.

The agreement worked. Congress asked President Washington to pick the capital's exact location. In 1791 he chose 10 square miles (26 sq km) of land straddling the

George Washington chose the site of the nation's capital city.

Potomac River. The new capital city would be called Washington, after President Washington.

On the site of the new city, there were only forests, swamps, and fields of corn and tobacco. Two small towns lay along the banks of the Potomac—Alexandria in Virginia and Georgetown in Maryland.

Although only a few farmers and townspeople lived in the District of Columbia in the 1790s, thousands of Native Americans, or American Indians, had once lived in the area. The Nanticoke, Piscataway, and Powhatan tribes had fished in the waters of the Potomac River and the Chesapeake Bay long before Europeans first came to the area in the early 1600s.

As European settlers arrived, they

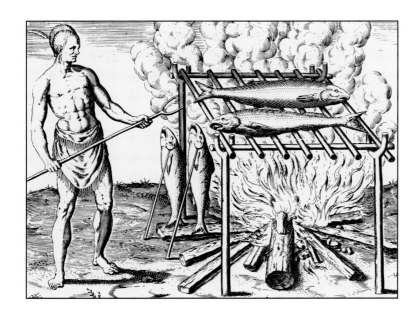

Powhatan Indians preserved fish by drying them over a fire.

gradually claimed more and more of the Indians' land. The settlers brought smallpox and other diseases with them. Native Americans had never been exposed to these illnesses, so thousands died.

To get away from European settlers, the Indians moved west and north. By 1791, when President Washington chose the site for the new capital, no Indians were left in the District of Columbia.

George Washington was no longer president when the U.S. government began moving to Washington, D.C., from Philadelphia, Pennsylvania, in 1800. That year a few government buildings in the new capital city were finished. But the rest of Washington was a mess.

The city's streets were not paved. Potholes and tree stumps made it dangerous to travel on horseback or in carriages—the main forms of transportation at that time. In dry weather, dust from the dirt roads filled the air. In rainy weather, the roads turned to mud.

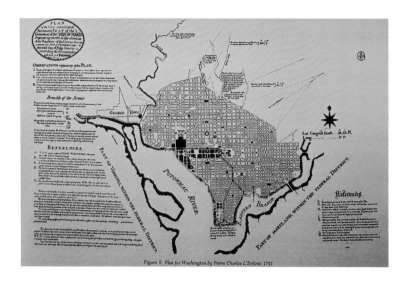

Figure 9. Plan for Washington by Pierre Charles L'Enfant, 1791

Pierre Charles L'Enfant, a French engineer, designed the nation's capital in 1791. He placed the Capitol building in the center of Washington.

In the early 1800s, farm animals freely wandered the streets of Washington, D.C.

Residents dumped their garbage into the streets, where some of it was eaten by roaming pigs. The capital was so rough and dirty that it was sometimes called "wilderness city."

The city was still unfinished in 1812, when the United States declared war on Great Britain. Great Britain had been fighting France for more than 10 years and was trying to prevent other countries, including the United States, from trading with France. British ships were also stopping U.S. ships on the Atlantic Ocean and forcing U.S. sailors to join the British navy.

On August 24, 1814, the British attacked Bladensburg, Maryland, a few miles northeast of Washington. In less than an hour, the British had defeated the U.S. soldiers who were protecting Washington. The Americans fled so quickly that the battle became known as the Bladensburg Races.

British soldiers marched into Washington the same night and set fire to the Capitol and the president's house. The next day, the British destroyed the Potomac bridge, the War and Treasury buildings, and the warehouses where weapons were stored.

Because the British ruined nearly all the government buildings in Washington, residents were afraid Congress would move the capital. But in February 1815, Congress voted to stay in Washington and rebuild the city. That same month, President James Madison signed a peace **treaty** with the British, ending the War of 1812.

During the War of 1812, British troops set fire to many of Washington's government buildings.

By 1820 Washington had become a slave-trading center. Government officials let traders keep slaves in Washington's jails while the traders waited to sell their slaves. Other traders held their slaves in pens set up along the National Mall.

Many people, particularly people who lived in Northern states, thought slavery was wrong. These people, called **abolitionists**, asked Congress to make slavery and the slave trade illegal in Washington. Abolitionists felt ashamed that people were bought and sold in the capital of a nation that claimed to give freedom and equality to everyone.

In 1850 Congress outlawed the slave trade in Washington. But the question of whether slavery—illegal in the North—should be legal in the South was still unsettled in 1860. That year, Abraham Lincoln was elected president of the United States.

Before being sold, slaves were held in prisons such as this one in Washington.

The Nation's Attic

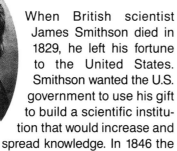

When British scientist James Smithson died in 1829, he left his fortune to the United States. Smithson wanted the U.S. government to use his gift to build a scientific institution that would increase and spread knowledge. In 1846 the U.S. Congress created the Smithsonian Institution. Since then the Smithsonian has been involved in many areas of study.

Joseph Henry, the institution's first secretary, helped organize regular weather reports in the United States. The institution also helped pay for expeditions to western North America. Explorers returned with animals they had caught and stuffed. Many explorers also brought back baskets, pottery, and other items made by Native Americans. These things became part of the Smithsonian's collection.

Nowadays the Smithsonian Institution is best known for its museums, several of which line the National Mall in Washington, D.C.

Visitors to the museums can see everything from the Hope Diamond—one of the world's most valuable diamonds—to the very first phones made by Alexander Graham Bell.

The museums also display paintings, sculptures, clothing, weapons, airplanes, books, space capsules, and prehistoric animal skeletons. Although millions of items are on display, only 1 percent of everything the Smithsonian owns can be shown at one time. With the nation's past stored in its warehouses, the Smithsonian has come to be known as the Nation's Attic.

A new dome was built on the Capitol during the Civil War.

Soon after Lincoln's election, 11 Southern states formed their own nation called the Confederate States of America, or the Confederacy. To preserve the United States, President Lincoln led the Union (Northern) army against the Confederate army in the Civil War, which began in 1861. Washington, D.C., sided with the Union.

One of the first important battles of the Civil War took place in July 1861, about 30 miles (48 km) from the District of Columbia near Manassas, Virginia. Washingtonians were sure the Northern army would win quickly. Many residents even took picnic lunches to watch the fight.

But the Northern army lost the battle. Wounded men walked or were carried in carts back to Washington. Those wounded at Manassas, as well as thousands of other Northern soldiers, were cared for in the capital's homes, schools, churches, and government offices. Doctors treated some soldiers in the Capitol building itself.

During the war, Washington's population grew rapidly. Many people came to start new businesses or to take government jobs related to the war. Thousands of slaves fled Confederate states and settled in Washington, where slavery was outlawed in 1862.

Families visited Union troops who were camped near Washington to protect the city during the Civil War.

Soon after the North won the war in 1865, slavery became illegal throughout the United States. That same year, Congress gave African American men the right to vote in the District of Columbia. In 1868 the residents of Washington elected John F. Cook and Carter A. Stewart to the city council. These men became the first African Americans to hold public office in the nation's capital, where one out of every three people were African American.

But in 1874, Congress changed Washington's form of government so that Washingtonians could no longer elect their own government representatives. Instead, the U.S. president chose just three people to run the district's government. Some white people were happy about this

Young people *(inset)* commonly worked long hours for very little pay in the bustling capital of the early 1900s *(lower left)*.

change because it meant that African Americans could no longer vote or be elected to the city's government.

At the beginning of the 1900s, Washington, D.C., was a bustling capital city. In 1901 more than 26,000 people worked for the U.S. government in Washington. Universities, museums, and even a national zoo had opened. But there was another side to the city. Thousands of poor people—many of them African Americans—lived along narrow alleys in crowded, run-down buildings.

31

In 1917, when the United States entered World War I, housing became a problem for thousands of new residents in the city. Many of these people had arrived in Washington to take wartime jobs with the U.S. armed forces or the American Red Cross. The U.S. government scrambled to quickly build lodgings.

About 10 years later, in 1929, an economic slump called the Great Depression hit the country. By 1932 one out of every four workers in the United States did not have a job.

To help end the depression, the U.S. government designed programs to put people throughout the country back to work. Thousands of jobs were created in Washington to run these programs. Most of the new government jobs went to white people. Many businesses stopped hiring African Americans altogether.

In the 1930s, Washingtonians in poor areas still did not have indoor plumbing.

The Hunger Marchers

Three years after the depression began in 1929, nearly 13 million Americans were out of work. Many people couldn't afford to buy enough food to feed their families. Known as the Hunger Marchers, large groups of unemployed people came to Washington to ask the U.S. government for help. Within a year, the U.S. government responded with programs that put Americans back to work and offered help to the needy.

Two Washingtonians search the paper for a job during the Great Depression.

In 1939 Marian Anderson was not allowed to sing in Washington's Constitution Hall because she was black. Angered by this decision, First Lady Eleanor Roosevelt arranged for Anderson to perform instead at the Lincoln Memorial.

In July 1941, 50,000 black people planned to come to Washington to protest the business practice of hiring only white workers. To prevent the march, President Franklin Roosevelt ordered the U.S. government to stop job discrimination, or the unfair treatment of workers because of their race.

But President Roosevelt's order did not stop job discrimination in private businesses. And his order did not prevent restaurants, hotels, and theaters from refusing to serve African Americans. It also did not stop colleges from refusing to allow African Americans to register for classes.

35

All these forms of discrimination led black people to begin a wave of protests in the 1950s in Washington and in other U.S. cities. Known as the **civil rights movement,** these protests resulted in the Civil Rights Act. Passed by Congress in 1964, this law forbids discrimination in public places such as hotels, parks, restaurants, and schools.

In 1963 civil rights leader Martin Luther King, Jr. *(inset, center),* **gave a famous speech about freedom and equality to a crowd of thousands** *(left)* **gathered at the Lincoln Memorial.**

37

The civil rights marchers were just one group of U.S. citizens who came to Washington to express their views and to seek help from Congress. Over the years, many different groups have come to the nation's capital to voice their feelings about many issues.

While many people come to the capital to be heard, Washington is the only city in the United States where residents do not have a full voice in their local government. From 1874 to 1973—nearly 100 years—residents of Washington, D.C., could not even elect their own government officials. In 1973 Congress voted to allow Washingtonians to elect a mayor and a city council. But Congress can still pass local laws and change any decision that members of the city government make.

Many Washingtonians want their local government to have the same powers that state governments have. In 1980 residents voted to make their city a state. Two years later, Washington's voters approved a state **constitution,** a document describing the basic laws of a state. Voters also agreed that their state would be called New Columbia.

The U.S. Congress has not approved Washington's constitution. But the city's residents have not given up. Many hope that someday soon Washington, D.C., will be a state as well as a capital city.

The Washington Monument *(tower, center)* and the Lincoln Memorial *(left of tower)* rise near the Capitol *(right of tower)* in Washington. Many residents hope the city will one day become a state.

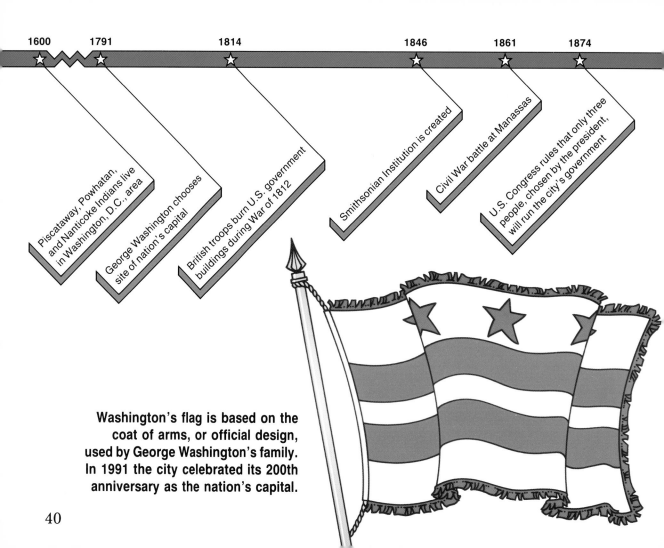

| 1600 | 1791 | 1814 | 1846 | 1861 | 1874 |

Piscataway, Powhatan, and Nanticoke Indians live in Washington, D.C., area

George Washington chooses site of nation's capital

British troops burn U.S. government buildings during War of 1812

Smithsonian Institution is created

Civil War battle at Manassas

U.S. Congress rules that only three people, chosen by the president, will run the city's government

Washington's flag is based on the coat of arms, or official design, used by George Washington's family. In 1991 the city celebrated its 200th anniversary as the nation's capital.

40

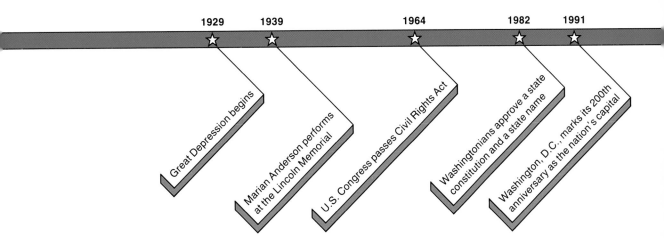

1929 — Great Depression begins

1939 — Marian Anderson performs at the Lincoln Memorial

1964 — U.S. Congress passes Civil Rights Act

1982 — Washingtonians approve a state constitution and a state name

1991 — Washington, D.C., marks its 200th anniversary as the nation's capital

Young Washingtonians have fun sledding down a hill.

A red and gold archway spans a street in Washington's Chinatown neighborhood.

42

Living and Working in Washington, D.C.

Washington, D.C., is home to 606,900 residents. But the population of the entire metropolitan area is much larger—3.9 million people. In the District of Columbia itself, two out of three people are African American—more than in most other cities in the United States. In the suburbs, only one out of five people are African American. Native Americans, Asian Americans, and **Latinos** make up a small percentage of the metropolitan area's population.

Children climb a dinosaur statue in front of the National Museum of Natural History.

43

Washington is also home to more than 40,000 people who are citizens of other countries. Some of these people are ambassadors, who represent foreign countries. Others work for international organizations such as the World Bank, which lends money to countries around the world.

Jobs with banks or with government organizations are called service jobs because they provide services to people or businesses. Most of Washington's service jobs are with the U.S. government—the largest employer in the Washington metropolitan area. The Department of Defense, for example, employs more than 20,000

Canadian flags fly outside the Canadian Embassy in Washington.

people. Altogether, about 589,000 people work for the U.S. government in the city and its suburbs.

Government employees do all kinds of jobs. Workers at the U.S. post office sort and deliver mail. Guards protect the city's many government buildings. The president of the United States and members of Congress work for the government, too.

After government, most service jobs are in tourism. Thousands of Washingtonians work in the city's hotels, restaurants, and travel agencies. These businesses offer services to the 20 million tourists who visit the capital city each year.

A guard at the Jefferson Memorial gives directions to a young man.

A giant globe lights up the office building where *National Geographic Magazine* is produced.

Some service organizations **lobby,** or work to influence, Congress. Lobbyists try to get laws passed that address the concerns of farmers, traders, manufacturers, and other groups. Organizations that lobby Congress hire lawyers, bookkeepers, secretaries, and others to help get the job done.

Other service workers in the capital include doctors, teachers, and salesclerks. Reporters write articles for Washington's newspapers and magazines. *USA Today,* a daily newspaper published in the metropolitan area, is read by people all over the world. Well-known magazines such as *National Geographic Magazine* and *U.S. News & World Report* are also published in the city.

About 100,000 Washingtonians hold construction jobs building roads, homes, and offices. Fewer workers—only 83,000—have jobs in manufacturing. Most of these people work for printing and publishing companies, where they print magazines, pamphlets, and other materials.

Construction workers put a statue in place.

Washington is known for its 17 universities and colleges, which include Georgetown, George Washington, and American universities. Howard University was founded in 1867 for the higher education of African Americans. Hearing-impaired students from all over the world come to study at Gallaudet University—the only college in the world for deaf people.

Students, residents, and tourists all enjoy Washington's many attractions. Some of the city's most popular sights are the Capitol building, the White House, the Washington Monument, the Lincoln Memorial, and the headquarters of the Federal Bureau of Investigation (FBI).

Visitors to the National Archives can see original copies of historical documents such as the U.S. Constitution, the Bill of Rights, and the Declaration of Independence. These valuable old papers are displayed in bronze and glass cases that can be lowered quickly into a special vault in case of a fire or other emergency. Tourists also enjoy watching sheets of dollar bills and postage stamps roll off the giant presses at the Bureau of Engraving and Printing.

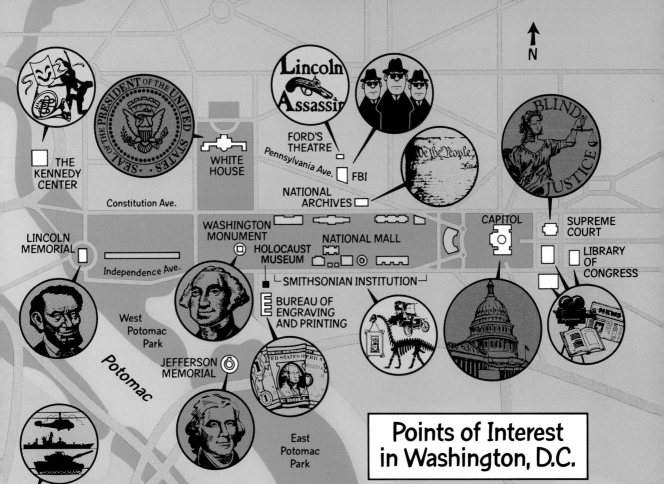

THE KENNEDY CENTER

SEAL OF THE PRESIDENT OF THE UNITED STATES

WHITE HOUSE

FORD'S THEATRE

Pennsylvania Ave.

FBI

NATIONAL ARCHIVES

SUPREME COURT

Constitution Ave.

LINCOLN MEMORIAL

WASHINGTON MONUMENT

NATIONAL MALL

CAPITOL

LIBRARY OF CONGRESS

HOLOCAUST MUSEUM

Independence Ave.

SMITHSONIAN INSTITUTION

BUREAU OF ENGRAVING AND PRINTING

West Potomac Park

JEFFERSON MEMORIAL

Potomac

East Potomac Park

PENTAGON

River

Anacostia R.

N

Points of Interest in Washington, D.C.

Visitors to the Vietnam Veterans Memorial place flowers next to the names of loved ones who died in the Vietnam War.

For lovers of museums and the arts, Washington, D.C., is a treasure trove. The many museums of the Smithsonian Institution, including the National Gallery of Art and the National Air and Space Museum, line the National Mall. Hundreds of priceless paintings hang in the art museum. Airplanes, rockets, and space capsules showing the history of air and space travel are featured at the National Air and Space Museum.

Theatergoers attend plays at the National Theater, Ford's Theatre, and Arena Stage. Concerts at the John F. Kennedy Center for the Performing Arts also draw many people. Sports fans buy hot dogs and watch the Washington Redskins football team score touchdowns in the Robert F. Kennedy Memorial Stadium. Fans enjoy watching the Washington Bullets shoot baskets and the Washington Capitals hockey team pass the puck in the metro area's Capital Centre.

Visitors to Washington, D.C., can enjoy a Washington Redskins football game (above) **and the National Air and Space Museum** (left).

The Chesapeake and Ohio Canal National Historical Park attracts outdoor enthusiasts. A 15-mile (24-km) stretch of the canal runs along the Potomac River from Georgetown to the river's Great Falls. The canal was built in the early 1800s to haul tons of coal to Washington. The path beside the canal is now a popular place to hike and ride bicycles. Visitors can also travel down the canal the way coal once did—in boats pulled by mules that walk along the waterway.

Rock Creek Park, which houses the National Zoological Park, is one of the largest woodland city parks in the world. The zoo's most famous resident is Hsing-Hsing, a giant panda given to the United

Mules pull a boat down the Chesapeake and Ohio Canal.

States by the People's Republic of China in 1972.

From its theaters and museums to its hiking trails and sports arenas, Washington, D.C., is just what a capital city should be—a place with something to interest everyone.

The panda at the National Zoological Park enjoys its lunch of bamboo.

Protecting the Environment

About 70 percent of the people who live in Washington's metropolitan area drive their cars to and from work. Many of these cars have air conditioners. On hot and muggy summer days, many drivers count on their air conditioners to make the ride more comfortable. But car air conditioners add to a serious environmental problem—the destruction of the **ozone** above the earth.

Ozone, a type of oxygen, forms a layer in the upper atmosphere high above the earth's surface. The ozone layer absorbs most of the sun's **ultraviolet (UV) radiation**. In large doses, these powerful rays from the sun can cause skin cancer and other health problems in humans and can harm and even kill plants and animals. UV radiation also can make paint crack more easily and can make plastics, rubber, and building materials wear out sooner.

Most working Washingtonians drive to their jobs.

TOMS total ozone

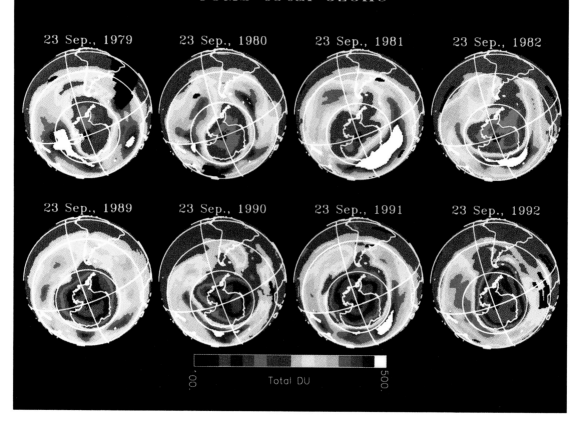

23 Sep., 1979   23 Sep., 1980   23 Sep., 1981   23 Sep., 1982

23 Sep., 1989   23 Sep., 1990   23 Sep., 1991   23 Sep., 1992

Total DU

Areas of blue or purple *(facing page)* show where ozone levels over Antarctica are low. The information was collected using special equipment aboard a satellite.

In 1985 scientists discovered a large area over Antarctica (the continent at the South Pole) where the ozone layer thins dramatically every spring. Three years later, in 1988, researchers announced that the ozone layer over the entire planet was thinning faster than most people had thought it would.

Chemicals called **chlorofluorocarbons (CFCs)** are the main substances that harm the ozone layer. These chemicals are used as the cooling fluid in refrigerators and air conditioners. When allowed to escape into the upper atmosphere, CFCs destroy ozone. When this happens, more UV radiation reaches the earth, threatening humans, plants, and animals.

Washington's famous cherry trees could be harmed by high levels of UV radiation.

57

Car air conditioners use more CFCs than most other products in the United States. Even when they are in good repair, car air conditioners leak CFCs. The chemicals also escape in auto accidents or when the air conditioners are being repaired.

Together with the governments of many other countries, the U.S. government in Washington, D.C., is working to save the ozone layer.

CFCs can leak when auto air conditioners are being repaired.

In 1987 the United States and about 80 other nations around the world signed an agreement called the Montreal Protocol. By signing this document, the participating nations agreed to cut the manufacture of CFCs in half by 1998. In 1990 these countries agreed to stop making CFCs altogether by the year 2000.

In its meetings in Washington, D.C., Congress has passed laws to stop manufacturing CFCs in the United States even before 2000. The laws also say that CFCs already in use must be recycled. For example, CFCs in refrigerators and air conditioners must be captured before the items are thrown away or junked, so that the CFCs can then be reused.

Safer chemicals are beginning to replace CFCs in motor vehicle air conditioners.

But the goals established by the Montreal Protocol and the U.S. Congress will be difficult to meet. The new laws, for example, are hard to enforce because it is not easy to catch people throwing out, instead of recycling, CFCs. And the equipment for capturing and recycling CFCs is expensive. Even if the goals are met, the ozone layer will not be safe for many years. Once CFCs escape into the upper atmosphere, they can destroy ozone for up to 100 years.

Getting rid of CFCs depends partly on ordinary people. Car owners in Washington, D.C., and other parts of the United States can help by making sure their auto mechanics recycle CFCs. The next time consumers buy a car, they can choose one without an air conditioner. And, as new models become available, buyers will be able to purchase a car with an air conditioner that doesn't use CFCs.

Even if you don't own a car, you can help save the ozone layer. Like a lobbyist, you can try to persuade Congress to pass laws that reduce air pollution. You can write to the politicians from your state to express your view. Together, the U.S. government in Washington and all of the nation's citizens can make the earth a healthier place to live.

Walking and riding bicycles instead of driving cars will help protect the earth's ozone layer.

Famous People from Washington, D.C.

ACTORS

Billie Burke (1885–1970) was born into a family of entertainers in Washington, D.C. A talented actress, Burke was well known for her roles on stage and in films. Her most famous role was that of Glinda the Good Witch in *The Wizard of Oz*.

Helen Hayes (1900–1993), a native of Washington, D.C., began her acting career when she was only five years old. As an adult, she acted in Broadway plays and starred in many films including *Airport,* for which she won an Oscar in 1970.

John Heard (born 1946) is an actor from Washington, D.C. He has appeared on stage and in many films, including *The Trip to Bountiful* and *Awakenings*.

▲ BILLIE BURKE

HELEN HAYES ▶

◀ WILLIAM HURT

William Hurt (born 1950) is a well-known stage and film actor. He has starred in numerous movies, including *The Big Chill, Broadcast News,* and *The Doctor*. In 1985 Hurt won an Oscar for his performance in *The Kiss of the Spider Woman*. Hurt is from Washington, D.C.

ELGIN BAYLOR ▶

ATHLETES

Elgin Baylor (born 1934) played basketball with both the Minneapolis Lakers and the Los Angeles Lakers. Born in Washington, D.C., Baylor has a career average of 27.4 points per game—one of the sport's highest averages.

Sugar Ray Leonard (born 1956) is a boxer known for his speed and clever footwork. Born into a family of boxers, Leonard won a gold medal at the 1976 Olympic Games. During his professional career, he has won world championship titles in five weight classifications, a distinction he shares with only one other professional boxer. Leonard is from Washington, D.C.

Maury Wills (born 1932), from Washington, D.C., played baseball for the Los Angeles Dodgers for most of his career. In 1962 Wills broke the record for stolen bases and was named the National League's Most Valuable Player. In the early 1980s, Wills was named manager of the Seattle Mariners, becoming one of the first African American managers in the major leagues.

▲ SUGAR RAY LEONARD

MAURY WILLS ▶

 ◀ ANN BEATTIE

MARJORIE KINNAN ▶ RAWLINGS

AUTHORS

Edward Franklin Albee, III (born 1928), is an award-winning playwright from Washington, D.C. Among his best-known works are *Who's Afraid of Virginia Woolf?*, *A Delicate Balance*, and *Seascape*.

Ann Beattie (born 1947) writes novels and short stories. Born in Washington, D.C., Beattie has contributed stories to well-known literary magazines such as *The New Yorker* and *Harper's*. In 1985 she wrote a book called *Spectacles* for young readers. Her novels include *Falling in Place* and *Picturing Will*.

Marjorie Kinnan Rawlings (1896–1953) was born in Washington, D.C. Rawlings gave up her career as a journalist to live on a farm in rural Florida, where she began to write fiction. Her best-known book, *The Yearling*, earned her a Pulitzer Prize in 1939.

Helen Van Slyke (1919–1979), a popular romance writer, grew up in Washington, D.C. After a successful career as a fashion editor and later as an advertising executive, Van Slyke turned to writing fiction. Her best-selling novels include *A Necessary Woman* and *No Love Lost.*

JOURNALISTS

Connie Chung (born 1946), an award-winning broadcast journalist, was born in Washington, D.C. In the 1980s, she anchored various NBC news programs. Since 1989 Chung has been with CBS, where she coanchors "The CBS Evening News" with Dan Rather.

▲ CONNIE CHUNG

JUDITH MARTIN ▶

◀ ROGER MUDD

Judith Martin (born 1938) is best known as "Miss Manners," the author of an advice column on etiquette (manners) that appears in newspapers across the country. Martin grew up in Washington, D.C.

Roger Mudd (born 1928), a journalist from Washington, D.C., has won several Emmy awards for his reporting. Mudd's career as a television news correspondent with CBS, NBC, and PBS has spanned more than 30 years.

MUSICIANS

Duke Ellington (1899–1974) was born in Washington, D.C. A piano player, Ellington became one of the most famous jazz composers and bandleaders of his time. He wrote more than 5,000 original works, including "Mood Indigo" and "Sophisticated Lady."

DUKE ELLINGTON ▶

Marvin Gaye (1939–1984), a singer and songwriter, was the son of a Washington minister. Gaye began his career singing with the choir at his father's church. Gaye's hits include "I Heard It through the Grapevine" and "What's Going On."

MARVIN GAYE ▶

John Philip Sousa (1854–1932) was a famous bandleader and composer born in Washington, D.C. Known as the March King, Sousa wrote more than 100 march tunes. His most famous is "Stars and Stripes Forever," a popular Fourth of July march.

Peter Tork (born 1944), originally from Washington, D.C., played bass guitar for the Monkees, a rock band popular in the 1960s. The group's hits included songs such as "Last Train to Clarksville" and "I'm a Believer."

PETER TORK ▶

▲ JOHN PHILIP SOUSA

POLITICAL LEADERS

Angela Marie Buchanan (born 1948), a native of Washington, D.C., served as treasurer of the United States from 1981 to 1983. She was the youngest person ever to hold the position.

John Foster Dulles (1888–1959), born in Washington, D.C., was a lawyer and diplomat. In 1945 Dulles helped create the United Nations, an organization that works for world peace.

▲ ANGELA MARIE BUCHANAN

▲ JOHN FOSTER DULLES

MARY ◀ AGNES CHASE (right)

SCIENTIST

Mary Agnes Chase (1869–1963), born in Illinois, moved to Washington, D.C., in 1903 to begin a 36-year career with the U.S. Department of Agriculture. Chase was known for her research on grasses.

Facts-at-a-Glance

Nicknames: Nation's Capital, Capital City
Motto: *Justitia omnibus* (Justice for All)
Flower: American beauty rose
Tree: scarlet oak
Bird: wood thrush

City population: 606,900*
Rank in city population, nationwide: 48th
Metropolitan area population: 3,923,574*
City area: 68 sq mi (176 sq km)
Metropolitan area: 3,957 sq mi (10,249 sq km)
Founded: 1791
U.S. senators: 1, nonvoting "shadow" senator
U.S. representatives: 1, nonvoting

*1990 census

Average January temperature: 37° F (3° C)   **Average July temperature:** 78° F (26° C)

66

Places to visit: U.S. Capitol building, the White House, Washington Monument, Capital Children's Museum, Hirshhorn Museum and Sculpture Garden, National Museum of Women in the Arts, Explorers Hall at the National Geographic Society, U.S. Holocaust Memorial Museum

Annual events: Chinese New Year Festival (Feb.), Cherry Blossom Festival (April), White House Spring Garden Tour (April), Potomac Riverfest (June), Caribbean Summer in the Park (July), Latin American Cultural Festival (July), National Frisbee Festival (Sept.)

WHERE WASHINGTONIANS WORK
Services—64 percent
    (services includes jobs in trade; community, social,
    & personal services; finance, insurance, & real
    estate; transportation, communication, & utilities)
Government—27 percent
Construction—5 percent
Manufacturing—4 percent

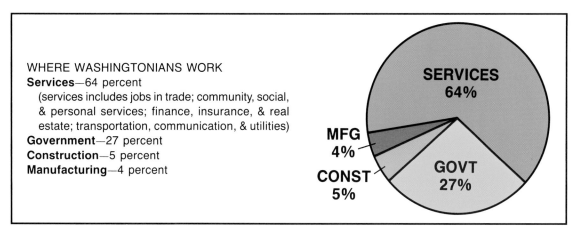

SERVICES 64%
MFG 4%
CONST 5%
GOVT 27%

Glossary

abolitionist   A person who works to abolish, or end, something. The term usually refers to the people who worked to abolish slavery before the Civil War.

chlorofluorocarbons (CFCs)   A group of chemicals that contain chlorine, fluorine, and carbon. CFCs are used as the cooling agent in air conditioners and refrigerators. In the upper atmosphere, CFCs destroy the earth's protective ozone layer.

civil rights movement   A movement to gain equal rights, or freedoms, for all citizens—regardless of race, religion, or sex.

constitution   The system of basic laws or rules of a government, society, or organization. The document in which these laws or rules are written.

Latino A person living in the United States who either came from or has ancestors from Latin America. Latin America includes Mexico and most of Central and South America.

lobby To try to influence lawmakers to pass laws that will benefit a certain group, company, or organization.

ozone A gas found in the earth's upper atmosphere, about 9 to 18 miles (14 to 29 km) above the earth's surface. Ozone in the upper atmosphere shields the earth from harmful rays from the sun. Ozone can also form as a poisonous gas in the earth's lower atmosphere, where the gas is considered air pollution.

precipitation Rain, snow, and other forms of moisture that fall to earth.

treaty An agreement between two or more groups, usually having to do with peace or trade.

ultraviolet (UV) radiation An invisible form of light released by the sun. UV radiation can also be produced artificially. In small doses, UV radiation helps kill germs and certain diseases. But in large doses, it can cause serious health problems.

Index

Acknowledgments:

Maryland Cartographics, Inc., pp. 2, 11; Pat Lanza / Folio, pp. 2–3; George Karn, p. 6; The White House, p. 7; Gene Ahrens, pp. 10, 39; Mae Scanlan, pp. 8, 12, 13, 41, 43, 46, 47, 55; Saul Mayer, pp. 14, 17; Jerry Hennen, pp. 16, 69; Library of Congress, pp. 19, 20, 21, 23, 26, 28, 29, 30, 31, 32, 33, 35; National Park Service, pp. 22, 45; Historical Society of Washington, D.C., Photo Collection, pp. 24–25; *Dictionary of American Portraits,* p. 27 (top left); Washington, D.C., Convention and Visitors Assoc., p. 27 (bottom right); National Archives, pp. 34 (#69–N–17200), 36–37 (#306–SSM–4B–80–10), 65 (top right #127–G–122H–A00320); UPI Photo, p. 36; Thomas Henion, pp. 42, 52, 67; Colette Champagne, p. 44; Richard Day, pp. 50, 51 (bottom left); © Scott Cunningham / Washington Redskins, p. 51 (top right); Anne B. Keiser, pp. 53, 57; NASA, p. 56; Wendy W. Cortesi, pp. 58, 70; Karelle Scharff, p. 59; Frederica Georgia, p. 61; Wen Roberts, p. 62 (bottom right); Hollywood Book & Poster Co., pp. 62 (top right and left, bottom left), 64 (bottom right), 65 (top center and left); UPI / Bettmann, p. 63 (top left); Los Angeles Dodgers, p. 63 (top right); Benjamin Ford, p. 63 (bottom left); University of Florida, Dept. of Special Collections, p. 63 (bottom right); Tony Esparza / CBS Photo, p. 64 (top left); United Feature Syndicate, Inc., p. 64 (top right); NBC Photo, p. 64 (bottom left); Angela "Bay" Buchanan, p. 65 (bottom left); State Dept., Technical Services Branch, p. 65 (bottom right); Hunt Institute for Botanical Documentation, Carnegie Mellon University, Pittsburgh, PA, p. 65 (bottom center); Jean Matheny, p. 66.